HOLIDAY

ALLEN EDWARDS

authorHOUSE®

AuthorHouse™ UK
1663 Liberty Drive
Bloomington, IN 47403 USA
www.authorhouse.co.uk
Phone: UK TFN: 0800 0148641 (Toll Free inside the UK)
    UK Local: 02036 956322 (+44 20 3695 6322 from outside the UK)

Published by AuthorHouse 07/15/2021

ISBN: 978-1-6655-9116-4 (sc)
ISBN: 978-1-6655-9115-7 (e)

PREFACE

My name is Allen Edwards, after retaking my English GCSE at evening classes, I discovered I had a passion and interest in creative writing and storytelling, as this was part of the English work and I had much to pass the exam I thought to myself I like doing this.

'Holiday' is inspired upon my own visit to Thailand back in 2014 whilst the events in this book are purely fictional, the hotel setting, some of the characters, in this book who are of different nationalities are based upon real people I met staying at my hotel. At the height of the COVID-19 pandemic in 2020 when the United Kingdom entered its first lockdown, like everyone else I had time to kill, especially in the evenings, with that I put pen to paper and wrote this book.

I came up with the idea of this story after asking myself the question: what would you do if you were on holiday and your partner was suddenly not there? Along with their belongings, passport etc and how would you react if the hotel staff claim to have not seen you're partner and claim you arrived alone?

PRELUDE

One late evening, on the outskirts of Bangkok, Thailand, a French man in his late 20s, a tourist, ran frantically down a dark quiet empty road, passing makeshift shacks and run-down buildings, a very apparent poor area of the city. The man startled when two stray dogs appeared in his way barking and growling at him. Frightened, he ran around the dogs, the dogs eyes followed him as he past them. Still running and tearful he put his phone to his ear. Speaking in French *'Dominique, Dominique! Please where are you?!* He said desperately.

Not looking where he was going he ran into a very busy road awash with cars and trucks. He stopped in the middle of the road and yelled in fear when a lorry's horn blew and its headlights edged closer towards him. Crash!! As the lorry failed to stop in time!

CHAPTER 1

In the living room of a flat in England, Mikey Morris was packing his sports bag ready for his game of rugby. He was a tall, slim, athletic man of 25 years of age who lived with his girlfriend Rachel Moore, a pretty woman two years younger. She sat looking on her phone. 'What time will you be home?' She asked Mikey,

'About six,' he replied,

'Are you actually though? Rachel asked. 'Because you always say you'll be back at a time, then don't.' she said.

'I defo will,' Mikey insisted. 'What are you looking at?' He asked,

'Just looking at the hotel we're staying at in Thailand,' replied Rachel, 'It looks nice,' she said.

'I know I can't wait to go, been looking forward to this trip for ages, only a week to go now,' said Mikey excitedly. Mikey grabbed his bag, 'I gotta go now babe' he said,

'Please don't be late' said Rachel,

'I won't, I'll play the game have a quick drink then I'll be home' promised Mikey. Mikey leant in and gave Rachel a quick kiss before leaving.

Rachel, knowing it was likely Mikey would break his promise, sat in doubt as he left.

Later that evening, in the early hours of the morning, Mikey in a very drunk state and soaked to the skin, staggered down the communal path in the pouring rain towards his front door. He clumsily fumbled his keys trying to open the door only to drop the keys on the floor. In the pitch black, Mikey knelt on the wet path, his hand splashed in rain puddles as he tried to look for the keys, eventually he found them, then let himself into the flat. Using the hallway wall as support he staggered towards the bathroom. Mikey collapsed down by the toilet, he put his head in the toilet and was very sick from the huge amount of drink he consumed.

Rachel asleep in the bedroom opposite the bathroom woke up to hear Mikey in the bathroom. She sat up and looked towards the bedroom door with tired eyes wondering what was going on. She walked into the bathroom to find Mikey passed out asleep on the bathroom floor, covered in his own sick, soaked to the skin and missing a shoe, his fellow rugby player and best mate Joe was trying to call him, Mikey too oblivious and drunk to notice his phone ringing let it ring constantly.

Mikey stirred as he saw Rachel stood in the doorway in her nightie looking very tired. 'Hey....sorry....I—,' he slurred. In an attempt to get up Mikey grabbed hold of the towel radiator to pull himself up, only to pull it off the wall. Crash! As he fell back to the floor and the towel radiator landed on top of him.

Rachel was shocked at what he'd just done. 'What are you doing!' she shouted,

'Oh shit......uh....I—,' groaned Mikey as he lay on the bathroom floor. Rachel slammed the bathroom door shut in anger.

The next morning, Mikey woke up on the bathroom floor, covered with plaster from where he pulled the towel radiator off the wall. He held his head and groaned in pain as he felt ill with a massive hangover. Mikey got up and made his way to the bedroom where he saw Rachel packing a suitcase. 'Hey, I'm really sorry—,'

'I don't wanna hear it, you're a joke Mikey! shouted Rachel as she continued to pack her case.

'Look Rach I—,'

'You can have this back, we are over!!' screamed Rachel taking off her expensive bracelet that Mikey bought her and throwing it at him.

'Rach please..,'

'I'm not interested in what you have to say,' shouted Rachel, 'How many more broken promises?'

'No Rach please just let me explain' pleaded Mikey. 'Explain what? One drink led to another? The boys wanted to go to town? I've heard it all before Mikey, you're full of shit!' snapped Rachel. Mikey said nothing as Rachel got tears in her eyes. 'You promise me you'd stop this, you promised you'd only stay for one but like always you get blind drunk and shit all over our relationship!'

'Look please I'm sorry' pleaded Mikey, 'Come on we're going away next week—'

'I don't want to go anywhere with you, 'interrupted

Rachel, 'you seriously think I want to go on holiday with you now?!' she said as she continued to gather her belongings.

'I'll do whatever it takes to prove to you how much you mean to me,' pleaded Mikey.

'How many times have I heard that before? snapped Rachel, 'So go on then, explain, what was so great about last night to get in such a state and shit all over our plans for today? Hey? Come on you wanted to explain? Was it another girl again?!! She asked.

This remark hit a nerve with Mikey, he gritted his teeth and edged closer to her, pointing his finger close to her face. 'Don't you fucking dare throw that in my face, no it wasn't!'

Mikey's towering height over Rachel and angry expression felt intimidating to her. 'Don't you threaten me, you horrible horrible person!' she shouted back,

'Well how about you stop fucking bringing that up for once, you miserable bitch!' shouted Mikey putting his fist through the wardrobe door, his punch put a hole in the door.

A silent stare of shock occurred between them as Rachel was horrified and frightened by his actions, Mikey instantly regretted what he'd done when he saw how frightened she was.

With tears in her eyes, Rachel grabbed her suitcase. 'Move out my way!!' She cried as she brushed past Mikey.

He followed her to the front door. 'No Rach please,'

'Leave me alone,' she cried.

'Rachel!!' Mikey cried as she stormed to the front door with her suitcase.

She stopped to open the front door, then looked back at Mikey stood in the hallway. 'I hate you!' she said with tears in her eyes, 'Why did you ever ask me to move in with you? I don't want to be with you, you're a nasty, selfish, horrible person!' She walked out slamming the door behind her. Rachel cried as she walked down the communal path from the flat. Mikey was shocked and upset at Rachel going. He slowly raised his hands to his head covering his eyes, he lowered his head and started to breathe heavy. In a state of shock, he slowly walked into the living room, he stood and stared aimlessly into the mirror on the wall. 'That's it mate you've blown it now!' he muttered to himself, 'No please Rach—give him another chance, he won't do it again.' He said to himself.

As the day, Mikey still upset with Rachel leaving him, sat there feeling glum, the flat was a mess, the bathroom was still a mess from where he hadn't cleared up the vomit or picked up the towel radiator. He text Rachel's phone, one of many he had sent throughout the day, all to no reply from her. Had he really blown it with Rachel this time?

CHAPTER 2

One week later. Mikey sat in a crowded aeroplane taking him to the holiday in Thailand, he looked down at Rachel sat next to him resting her head on his chest as she slept. Mikey rested his chin lovingly on her head as he gazed out the plane window and watched the sunrise lighting up the clouds a beautiful colour of gold.

Rachel woke up to the sound of the captain of the plane making an announcement to the passengers over the tannoy. 'Did you sleep? she asked Mikey, 'No, too uncomfortable,' he replied 'Shouldn't be long till we land now though.'

The Boeing 787 landed on the runway at Bangkok Suvarnabhumi Airport in the bright sunshine with a sudden thud, 'Oh my god!' gasped Rachel as the wheels of the plane hit the tarmac.

The plane taxied over to the gate. Mikey stood up to stretch, being over six feet tall he was glad to finally stand after such a long flight with little legroom. He opened the overhead cabinet for Rachel's handbag. Patiently the couple waited, and waited, till Mikey got a little bit frustrated as to why a family were struggling to find something in their hand luggage, the family were oblivious to the crowd of passengers they were holding up, even the air stewards were wondering why the crowd of passengers weren't moving, finally, the family finished what they were doing, Mikey watched as the teenage boy of the family got out a pair of headphones. 'No matter where you go on holiday there's always some gormless person holding everyone up.' remarked Mikey.

This sudden remark caused Rachel to burst out laughing.

'What?' Mikey asked. The crowd of passengers disembarked down the stairs, until it was the couple's turn to leave the plane. They were instantly hit by the bright hot sunshine as they stepped outside and made their way to arrivals. The two were overwhelmed by the noise of airport tugs and luggage carts moving about the tarmac, the deafening sound of other planes coming into land or leaving the airport, the heat was overwhelming for the pair as they naively arrived wearing winter clothes as it was a cold November when they left England and did not expect Thailand to be so hot upon arrival. 'Bloody hell it's 10:30 in the morning and already 30 degrees!' said Mikey as he checked the weather app on his phone.

Mikey & Rachel waited at the conveyor belt for their shared suitcase. Minutes went by, the crowd grew larger, still the conveyor belt didn't move. 'Oh what's taking so long!' complained Rachel, all hot and bothered.

'I don't know!' replied Mikey drenched head to toe in sweat. A sudden jolt sounded as the conveyor belt began to move, 'Oh finally!' said Rachel.

Mikey and Rachel arrived at passport control, to add further to their frustration the queue of tourists for passport control stretched as far as the eye could see. To make matters worse only two desks were open. Finally, it was their turn when Mikey & Rachel went to separate desks showing their passports to the immigration officers.

Then Mikey & Rachel stood outside the airport with their suitcase amongst the noise of planes landing, the smog of vehicle traffic added to the already hot temperature. In front of them stood a colossal jungle of concrete and steel pillars, roadways, metal walkways, and bus stops, packed with people coming and going. Mikey tried to wave down a taxi in the heavy traffic going back and forth past the airport entrance, but to no joy. 'Mikey just wave down a taxi!' demanded Rachel,

'What do you think I'm trying to do! snapped Mikey. A taxi pulled over for them, Mikey looked to Rachel with a sigh of relief when the taxi stopped.

On route to the hotel, the taxi turned off the main road down a quiet empty back street, not too far away from the airport. The street was awash with makeshift shacks and run-down buildings, Mikey was puzzled as to where they were going. Suddenly the taxi came to an abrupt stop, nearly sending Mikey and Rachel off their seat. The taxi driver without explanation got out then made his way round to the back passenger door, 'What's going on!' asked Rachel nervously, Mikey unsure was unable to answer her. The taxi driver opened their door, the couple nervously got out. To their relief, they were at their hotel. They paid the taxi driver as he gave them their suitcase from the boot.

Mikey carried their shared suitcase walked into the hotel with Rachel. The couple couldn't believe their eyes to see how spotless and immaculate the hotel was considering they didn't pay an expensive amount of money for it and given how it was in what looked like a rough neighbourhood. As they made their way to the reception desk they were greeted by Chanchai, the hotel concierge, he was a smartly dressed, slender man in his late 20s. He greeted Mikey & Rachel with a welcoming smile as they arrived at the counter. 'Hello we have a reservation with you,' said Mikey, Rachel was impressed by how nice the hotel was.

'Yes sir, name please?' responded Chanchai in a heavy Thai accent.

'Mikey Morris,' replied Mikey,

'Passports please' asked Chanchai. Mikey handed over his passport, Chanchai took it then checked Mikey and Rachel into the hotel. He handed back Mikey his passport and a room key. 'Hope you enjoy your stay,' he said with a welcoming smile. 'Thanks' replied Mikey.

Mikey and Rachel walked along the hotel corridor looking for their hotel room. '304, 304, 304 where are you?' Mikey said to himself looking for the room, 'Are we on the right floor?' asked Rachel,

'I think so.' replied Mikey. As they continued to search, they saw Sinh, a scruffy dressed hotel cleaner, a short plump man in his mid-50s with terrible burn scars to his face, he came out of a room pushing a cleaning trolley. Mikey couldn't help but notice, with that the two made eye contact and briefly engaged in an awkward stare as they passed one another till Mikey quickly turned away and found his hotel. 'Ah here we are Rach,' he said.

Mikey fell backwards onto the bed, Rachel walked over

to the window and gazed down at the hotel pool below reflecting in the sunshine. 'I am knackered' said Mikey,

'I just want to sleep!' replied Rachel. Mikey got up and walked over to Rachel, he stood behind her wrapping his arms around her. 'I'm so glad we're finally here, been looking forward to this for months,' he said, Rachel turned around and said seriously 'Don't think we're sorted, you still need to prove to me you're willing to put us first and not—,'

'I will I swear it,' promised Mikey.

The young couple looked into each other's eyes before having a hug.

Mikey & Rachel lay snuggled up in the bed asleep. Mikey woke up first, he kissed Rachel's head, she woke up too and cuddled Mikey, he slowly stroked her long dark hair.

'What time is it?' she asked,

'7' replied Mikey checking the time on his phone.

'Go to the restaurant and get us some tea,' joked Rachel,

'Nah you go,' replied Mikey,

'Can't, I'm too comfy,' she said. Mikey lay down next to Rachel, the two kissed and embraced passionately without a care in the world.

'Come on we better get up,' said Rachel getting out of bed 'Going for a shower,' she said walking to the bathroom. Mikey sat up in bed and turned on the TV, he flicked through the channels before settling with the channel BBC World Service. He listened as the newsreader told of military intervention against a terror groups on the Thailand/Malaysia border. Wondering what was taking Rachel so long Mikey walked over to the bathroom, he opened the door and to his surprise, Rachel wasn't in there! Mikey was confused as the light was off, the shower wasn't running and the towels were still folded as if no one had been in the bathroom at all! Mikey couldn't get his head around what was going on until 'BOO!' said Rachel coming out from hiding behind the door,

'Bloody hell!' said Mikey, 'I thought you'd vanished!'

'Haha, I got you a good one there,' joked Rachel,

'No you didn't,' said Mikey trying to cling to his pride.

Mikey walked out of the bathroom and picked up a piece of paper containing the hotel's WiFi code and his phone, Rachel followed 'What are you doing?' she asked as she dried herself off,

'WiFi,' replied Mikey connecting his phone, 'WiFi code is here,' he said putting the piece of paper down. Mikey sat down, his phone pinged constantly as it connected to the WiFi. Rachel looked over to Mikey. 'Bloody hell who's that?' asked Rachel. 'Group chats, all the messages have just come through now,' replied Mikey looking at his phone.

'I hope you not gonna be glued to that the whole time we're here,' said Rachel 'It's bad enough when we're home!'

'No I won't be,' replied Mikey,

'Are you getting ready?' asked Rachel,

'Yes' replied Mikey as he got up.

Mikey and Rachel having dressed in some cooler clothes entered the hotel restaurant, a big open room opposite the hotel bar with only a few other hotel guests in there, they sat at a table. Love, a smartly dressed waiter from India, of thin stature, in his mid 20s came over 'Good evening' he said politely as he handed them the menus, Mikey spotted his name tag. Love left them while they looked at the menus. 'Did you see his name?' asked Mikey smirking,

'No why?' replied Rachel,

'His names 'Love,' laughed Mikey, Rachel didn't take much interest in Mikey's comment. 'You having a drink?' She asked him,

'Yeah what beers do they have,' said Mikey looking at the drinks page,

'Really?' asked Rachel as Mikey always had an alcoholic drink no matter where he went.

'Why not?' he replied, 'We're on holiday, you having one?'

'I only want a soft drink,' replied Rachel.

Whilst the couple sat in the restaurant a smartly dressed Thai man in his mid 40s dressed walked into the hotel. Chanchai came from behind the bar to greet him smiling and laughing the two men hugged each other. The man spoke in Thai *Hello old friend,*' he said to Chanchai. Mikey sat at his table noticed the man in the suit. The man glanced over at Mikey and Rachel's table making eye contact with Mikey, Mikey quickly turned his head before the man headed off with Chanchai into the office behind the reception desk. Mikey & Rachel continued looking at the menu. Love walked over to their table, 'You ready order sir?' He asked, speaking in a strong Indian accent.

On the way back to their room, Mikey & Rachel laughed and spoke about their times as children when they spotted Sinh the cleaner they saw earlier sat at the foot of the staircase murmuring to himself cradling a near-empty bottle of whisky. Sinh awakened by their laughter and made eye contact with Mikey. He got up and stumbled towards them,

'*What you laughing at American! You got problem American?*' shouted Sinh in Thai.

Mikey and Rachel both looked at each other confused as to what he was saying when suddenly Sinh started waving his whisky bottle aggressively at Mikey. Rachel horrified by what was happening hid behind Mikey, Mikey struggled to understand Sinh as he continued to shout at him in Thai and wave his whisky bottle at him, they backed off slowly, Mikey held his hands in the air indicating he didn't want any trouble, 'Wow ok mate we don't want any trouble!' He said trying to defuse the situation,

'*Don't like you American, I kill you!*' Sinh shouted at them in Thai,

Mikey and Rachel both petrified continued to back away from him till Love the waiter appeared, he spoke in Thai to Sinh ordering him to leave them alone. Sinh slowly turned towards Love, who ordered him to go home, Sinh stumbled away murmuring to himself. Love turned to a nervous Mikey and Rachel. 'I sorry,' apologised Love, Mikey was furious

'We didn't do anything he just—,'

'He from Vietnam,' interrupted Love, 'He think anyone speak English American,'

Mikey was baffled by what Love just said, 'We're not American!' said Mikey.

'He no know that he troubled please accept my apology.' said Love.

Mikey and Rachel still quite shaken walked into their hotel room. 'What the hell was his problem!' said Rachel,

'I don't know!' Mikey replied,

'Why do they employ such a man?' said Rachel,

'He's obviously very drunk,' answered Mikey,

'I'm not comfortable with him coming in here to clean not after that!' said Rachel,

'I know, we'll put all the valuables in here, he won't be able to get in here,' said Mikey putting both their passports and money in the safe. He then looked in the fridge for a drink then closed it when there was none. 'I'm going to get some water from the shop,' he said 'I won't be long.'

Mikey walked back to the hotel carrying some bottled water. He observed the makeshift houses, the rubbish, the poverty as he walked along the road, not a soul as was about, an unnerved silence stayed with him as he walked on alone. The nervousness was soon confirmed when some stray dogs from the shacks appeared in his path barking and growling at him. Mikey nervously edged away, but every small step brought the dogs closer, snarling and scrunching their noses at him. Mikey slowly stepped to the side. The dogs didn't take their eyes off him. He managed to get behind them, slowly edging away, backwards, keeping his eyes locked on them until the dogs eventually lost interest in him before wandering off in a different direction, Mikey without hesitation ran back to his hotel.

Back at the hotel, Mikey walked up to his hotel room door, he paused with worry when he saw the door was open slightly. Fearing the worst that an intruder had got into his hotel room he barged the door open, only to startle Rachel sat on the bed. 'Bloody hell what you doing?' She said alarmed,

'The door was open!' said Mikey.

'You must have left it open,' Rachel assumed.

'I thought—,'

'Thought what?' asked Rachel.

'Nothing.' said Mikey closing the door.

CHAPTER 3

The next day, Mikey and Rachel took the sky train into Bangkok, they observed the city around them as the train sped down the track. As the train got further into Bangkok, it ran parallel to one of the many motorways which led into the city and beyond, Mikey spotted a man riding scooter down the busy carriageway carrying his wife and toddler child, although he only saw them briefly, Mikey was astonished to see they didn't appear to wear any crash helmets or anything. 'Did you see that?' He asked Rachel.

First, they visited a crowded busy marketplace, being over 6 feet tall, Mikey towered above the locals. He picked two shot glasses with Thailand slogans on them from a stall 'Hey what do you think about this?' asked Mikey, he turned to see what Rachel thought only for her to no longer be there! Mikey turned his head looking in all directions for her, but he couldn't see her, Mikey placed the item down and began to look for Rachel, where had she gone? The huge crowd of people made it hard for Mikey to see her. After minutes of searching Mikey began to worry, all thoughts ran through his mind, had Rachel wandered off and got lost? Had he not been paying attention to where she said she might have gone? Mikey just didn't know! As he was about to get more worried he heard a familiar voice call his name 'Mikey!' He turned around to see Rachel stood with her hands on her hips with a face of thunder. 'Where have you been!' She said,

'Where have you been?' asked Mikey, 'I was showing you something and you disappeared!'

'What?' asked Rachel who was baffled, 'I said I wanted to look over there! You need to—,'

'Alright, alright,' interrupted Mikey, 'You're here now let's go.'

Next, Mikey and Rachel visited the Baiyoke Tower II, one of the highest buildings in Bangkok. As the pair approached it, they were dwarfed by the surrounding skyscrapers in the city centre, seeing so many, this briefly reminded Mikey of his trip to New York. The pair entered the Baiyoke Tower II, from there they got a elevator to the top floor, they both admired the view of Bangkok below, smothered in the smog of pollution and humidity, the pair laughed and joked with each other as they took selfies on Rachel's phone, as well as taking some photos of the view itself. Rachel handed a tourist her phone to take a photo of her and Mikey arm in arm with the view behind them, the two smiled very happily as their photo was taken.

Next, they visited the Golden Temple in the city. The golden domes and spires of the temple glistened in the sunshine, Mikey and Rachel, just like their fellow tourist took many photos on their phones amongst the busy crowds of tourists, before Rachel took a lovely selfie of them both amongst the stunning and beautiful architecture.

Finally, they visited the Lying Buddha statue, Rachel laughed as she tried to take a photo of Mikey lying down next to the statue, trying to copy the Lying Buddha, Mikey's funny antics even caused fellow tourists to laugh as well. Finally, after getting a photo, Mikey leapt up and kissed Rachel. The happiness between the young lovers couldn't be any stronger.

Later that evening, Mikey and Rachel sat at a table on a river cruise having just finished their dinner. The city's bright lights reflected beautifully off the calm smooth millpond Chao Phraya River. 'Come on let's have another.' said Rachel getting her phone out, they leaned in closer to each other smiling for the camera, Rachel tried to get a selfie of them both but to no avail. 'Oh can you do it, you got longer arms than me,' asked Rachel,

'Leave it to the pro,' said Mikey taking Rachel's phone. He took a selfie of them both before they both sat back. Rachel placed her hand on Mikey's hands. 'I've had a really nice day today,' she said happily, before taking a sip from her soft drink.

'Me too it's been special,' said Mikey as he picked up his bottle of Budweiser for a swig.

'I don't mean to keep bringing it up but before we come here our relationship was in a bad way but this has just proved to me how strong and special it really is,' said Rachel 'Everything that's gone on before I can forget all that now knowing special things really are.' she added.

'It's fine,' replied Mikey, 'I meant what I said before

we left how much I wanted to prove things to you and how much I was willing to try.' He added holding Rachel's hand too.

'And that you have,' Rachel replied 'I know it's only the second day but already you have proven to me and have more than tried, it's been wonderful,' she added.

'I love you,' said Mikey 'I don't want us to break up I really really want this,' he said gently rubbing his thumb over her hand.

'I know, I want it too, and I love you too,' said Rachel, the pair leaned into each other for another kiss.

Back at the hotel, Mikey and Rachel entered their hotel room kissing. Mikey kicked the door closed behind him, they edged closer to the bed kissing, he rubbed his hands up Rachel's back enjoying the moment of intimacy before pulling himself away. 'Umm I gotta go to the loo,' said Mikey feeling slightly embarrassed at having to interrupt the moment briefly.

'No you can wait' insisted Rachel as she carried on kissing her boyfriend and tried to undress him.

'No no I need I'm bursting,' laughed Mikey awkwardly.

'Ok we'll hurry up,' demanded Rachel running her hand down Mikey's torso. Mikey threw his phone on the bed then ran into the bathroom. Rachel lay on the bed, she lifted her dress slightly higher revealing more of her leg whilst waiting for Mikey. While she waited, Mikey's phone pinged with a message, she picked up the phone and saw Mikey had a message from his best friend Joe. She opened it. The message read: 'Alright gayboy I bought those tickets for Scotland England game will look at hotels later send us money when you can cheers gay.' Rachel annoyed at what she just read put the phone down. Mikey walked back in from the bathroom, Rachel looked at him. 'You had a message,' she said,

'It can wait,' replied Mikey as he moved closer to Rachel hoping to carry on the moment of intimacy. 'Off Joe,' she replied backing away from Mikey 'Going to Scotland are you?' She asked. Mikey stopped and read the message.

'Ohh, yeah we talked about this a while ago,' said Mikey sheepishly, Rachel sat up.

'Why do I have to find out like this?' She said 'Why didn't you tell me you were planning a trip to Scotland?!'

'I was going to tell when I knew for definite we were going.' explained Mikey.

'Poor excuse!' Said Rachel, 'This is what I been saying for ages how you don't tell me anything! Why do I have to keep finding out through other people when you and Joe are doing something? And why am I finding this out on our holiday!?' She said.

'Come on I don't wanna fall out over this we've had a great day—,'

'Then why does this keep happening then!!' Interrupted Rachel, 'We can't even be the other side of the world without you and Joe arranging a trip!' Mikey tried to play it down,

'I promise I was going to tell you,' he explained.

'Just like you promise this holiday would be a fresh start for us, for our relationship!?' said Rachel by now she had a tear in her eye. 'I thought today we'd put everything behind us, I thought we'd really made a fresh start. But it's obvious things will never change!' She said feeling hurt.

'Things have changed just because I want to go away

with Joe for a weekend doesn't mean I don't value our relationship,' explained Mikey

'But don't value it enough to tell me you're going?' She asked, Rachel went and stood by the window upset looking out with her back to Mikey.

'I do value us!' Mikey pleaded standing behind her. 'You didn't seem to value us last time you went away with Joe!' snapped Rachel,

'What? No!' snapped Mikey, 'Rachel you cannot keep bringing that up, yes I did fuck up but I'm not gonna do it again, we both agreed to put that behind us.' He said. Rachel turned and faced him.

'It's really hard to believe you when you can't even tell me you're going away.' She said, 'We might have sorted it but it still hurts, I can't forget just like that,' she added. Mikey annoyed at her for bringing a past incident involving him and another woman snapped back at Rachel.

'Oh for Christ sake, why can't you let that go? Yes I'm sorry you had to find out this way but I'm not having you constantly bring up what I did!!'

'Go on lose your shit again, you gonna put your fist through that door as well?' argued Rachel. Mikey said nothing, he gritted his teeth in anger and glared at Rachel before walking to the hotel room door.

'Where are you going?' Rachel asked,

'Be on my own,' he replied,

'Do nothing about us like you always do?' said Rachel,

'Hey maybe I'd tell you these things sooner if for once you didn't always fucking kick off!!' shouted Mikey opening then slamming the door shut behind him.

Mikey sat at the hotel bar holding a bottle of Budweiser feeling glum. Love was serving behind the bar. 'Would you like another drink sir?' He asked Mikey, Mikey shook his head in response and continued to sit there when Alex, a smartly dressed, bubbly, friendly Australian woman, of 42 years of age, with shoulder-length wavy blonde hair, carrying her suitcase arrived, she came up to the bar. 'Hi can I get a vodka tonic please?' She said to Love behind the bar, she noticed Mikey,

'You in transit?' She asked,

'Sorry?'

'You in transit here?' She asked again. Mikey who was not in the mood for conversation grunted his replies.

'No.'

'Ahh ok, visited my sister in London and this place is popular for people in transit.' Alex explained,

'I'm here for couple of weeks.' replied Mikey slouched at the bar holding his bottle of booze.

'That long?' She asked, 'Wow, may see ya around, being the silly cow I am missed my connecting flight home can't get another for two days,' she laughed. Mikey not in the mood for conversation said nothing. 'You here on your own?' Alex asked him,

'Missus is upstairs.' He replied.

'And your down here? She asked him, to which he nodded his head.

'Oh I see lovers spat eh, that explains why ya look glum,' said Alex,

'Is it obvious?' said Mikey sarcastically.

'Oh yes' said Alex, 'You won't find the solution in that

mate!' She advised, hinting at Mikey's drink. 'Just wanted a drink,' he explained,

'Take my advice, nip it in the bud soon otherwise the vacation gets remembered for all the wrong reasons,' Alex advised,

'Yeah will do,'

'Do it, I'm Alex by the way,' she said introducing herself.

'Mikey,' he replied,

Alex took her drink and turned to walk off.

'May ya see round Pom.' She joked before leaving Mikey alone. Mikey pondered for a minute then decided to go back and patch things up with Rachel, he took one last swig of his drink then left the hotel bar.

Mikey walked back into his hotel room, he walked in and to his surprise, Rachel was not there! The TV was on but Rachel was nowhere to be seen! He got out his phone and text her: 'Where are you?' Mikey very puzzled about her whereabouts sat on the end of the bed, he struggled to keep his eyes open as he hadn't quite adjusted to the time difference yet and had a very busy tiring day exploring Bangkok. The TV was left on the channel BBC world service which repeated the story of military intervention against terror groups on the Thailand/Malaysia border. He checked his phone to see if Rachel had replied, but she hadn't. Mikey really struggled to fight the exhaustion as his head kept nodding forwards in tiredness, unable to fight it anymore he collapsed backwards and fell asleep.

CHAPTER 4

The next morning, Mikey woke up, he quickly looked to see if Rachel was there, but she wasn't. Immediately he checked his phone, but had no message from Rachel, he tried to ring her only for his phone to say 'call failed' his phone network meant he couldn't use the phone abroad. He tried Facebook messenger in the hope Rachel would at least see that if she had some WiFi somewhere.

Mikey looked around by the hotel pool, the sun loungers around the hotel restaurant too, again there was no sign of Rachel. Next, he went outside the hotel and looked in both directions up the road, now very confused as to where Rachel could be Mikey set off looking for her, passing the run-down buildings and makeshift shacks, the same ones he passed two nights previous where he encountered the stray dogs, Mikey braced himself as he passed the area where they appeared that night, but thankfully the dogs didn't appear.

At the top of the road from the hotel, Mikey came to the busy six-lane main road, which he travelled along from the airport, busy and noisy with trucks, scooters, buses and cars hurtling along in both directions, he walked along where he came to a shop window where he stopped and looked in for

Rachel, he looked for her in a small market place, all to no joy. Mikey walked along the main road which ran parallel to the airport runway. Mikey stopped and looked all directions for any sign of Rachel, with the busy main road going on for miles in both directions he didn't know which way to go, he decided to try the hotel again, to see if she'd come back.

Mikey returned to his hotel room to see if Rachel had come back, to his disappointment she wasn't there. He checked his phone to see if she had replied but she hadn't, he tried ringing again with no success, Mikey began to worry 'Fucking hell Rach where the hell have you gone!' He said to himself. Mikey checked the hotel restaurant again for Rachel, but she wasn't there either. Alex was in the restaurant, she left her table having just finished breakfast when she spotted Mikey stood there looking puzzled. 'Oh hello again everything alright?' She asked him, Mikey showed her a photo of Rachel on his phone.

'Have you seen her at all?' He asked,

'No, is that your girlfriend?' Alex replied,

'Yeah.'

'She's pretty, no I haven't,' she said,

'Damn,' uttered Mikey looking around with an apparent look of worry.

'Is everything alright?' Alex asked him,

'No I—,'

'When you see her last?' Alex asked him,

'Last night,'

'Last night?' said Alex quite surprised,

'Yes.' said Mikey quite embarrassed. Alex suggested

Mikey ask Love who was behind the bar, he went over to him. 'Excuse me,' he said to Love,

'Yes sir' Love replied,

'Don't suppose you've seen my girlfriend in here have you?' Mikey asked showing Love the photo of Rachel on his phone, Love shook his head,

'No I no see her,' he said,

'Damn, ok' sighed Mikey.

Alex came over to him 'Any joy?' She asked, Mikey shook his head, 'Have you looked for her?' She asked him,

'All morning,'

'Where have you looked?'

'All over,' replied Mikey 'I can't find her anywhere, my phone won't even ring hers.'

'Do you wanna try mine? I got international calls,' offered Alex,

'Oh yeah please that be great,' said Mikey grateful. Mikey called Rachel off Alex's phone only for that to say 'call failed'.

'Ahhh this doesn't work either!' said Mikey now quite anxious,

'Oh I don't know then,' said Alex 'Let's start from the beginning when did you last see her? What's her name as well?' She asked him,

'Rachel, last night before I came down here,' said Mikey,

'Was she in the room when you got back?' asked Alex,

'No.' replied Mikey,

'Did you look for her?' She asked,

'No I...' Mikey hesitated to answer,

'What?'

'I dozed off,' said Mikey sheepishly,

'Dozed off!?' asked a baffled Alex, Mikey began to panic

'I text her, I dozed off next thing I know it's morning and she's still not there I feel stupid for doing so I wish I—,'

'Alright alright calm down calm down, we'll ask around some more someone's bound to of seen her,' said Alex kindly to reassure him. Mikey agreed, Mikey gets the photo of Rachel again, Alex took a photo of the photo of Rachel. She went around the tables asking guesses if they had seen her, Mikey asked Chanchai on the reception desk. 'Excuse me have you seen this girl?' He asked showing Chanchai the photo of Rachel,

'No sir,' he said shaking his head.

'Are you sure?' asked Mikey by now getting frustrated.

'Yes is she guest here?' asked Chanchai,

'Yes we checked in here together two days ago,' replied Mikey 'You checked us in.' He added.

'Please I get my boss.' said Chanchai.

Chanchai disappeared into the office behind the desk to get the hotel manager, Alex came over to Mikey.

'Any joy?' She asked,

'No, he's getting his boss.' said Mikey,

'No one over there has seen her,' said Alex 'A lot of them only arrived here today.' Chanchai and Wirat a man in his mid 40s the hotel manager came out of the office. 'Can I help you sir?' He asked Mikey, 'Have you seen this girl?' asked Mikey showing the manager the photo of Rachel.

'No sir is she guest here?'

'Yes,' replied Mikey.

Wirat spoke in Thai to Chanchai. 'This is turning into a frigging nightmare!' said Mikey,

'She can't be far, we'll keep checking' said Alex. Wirat

finished speaking to Chanchai. 'My colleague says he remembers checking you in the hotel' he said,

'Right?'

'But you were alone.' said Wirat.

Mikey was puzzled by the managers claim.

'What!?'

'My colleague say you were alone.' Wirat repeated,

'Wait, no no Rachel was with me' claimed Mikey,

'I checked you in alone sir' said Chanchai. Mikey and Alex both looked at each other very puzzled. 'No she was with me I tell you, you must remember her,' asserted Mikey,

'Sorry sir no,' insisted Chanchai,

'Who's name is the booking under?' asked Alex,

'Mine,' said Mikey, 'She was with me we both checked in here, we ate in that restaurant! Your colleague over there served us!' He insisted pointing towards Love. Wirat went over to Love. 'What are they playing at?' said Mikey,

'He probably can't remember, loads of people check-in and out of here,' said Alex, Wirat and Love both come over to Mikey and Alex.

'My colleague says he only served you,' said Wirat, Mikey was more shocked at what all the hotel staff were saying, whilst Alex look confused at both Mikey's and the staff's different theory's. 'What? You served the both of us two nights ago!' said Mikey,

'Only you sir.' insisted Love,

'What did you order Mikey?' asked Alex,

'I had Thai green curry, Rachel had…I can't remember, she was sat opposite me!' He said,

'I only serve you sir.' insisted Love,

'You didn't!' insisted Mikey. Chanchai typed into the computer

'Your name please?' He asked Mikey,

'Mikey Morris.' Mikey replied,

Chanchai typed in the details on the computer, he then showed Wirat, he looked at the computer then turned the screen to show Mikey his reservation.

'Sir your reservation with us is only for one,' he said, Mikey looked at the computer, he could not believe his eyes, he was horrified to see the computer confirmed this. Alex looked at it too then looked at Mikey all confused.

'Says you only reserved it for one?' She said, Mikey couldn't believe what he was seeing.

'No that's not possible I—,'

'Please sir,' interrupted Wirat 'My colleague say they only see you here, the computer confirms only you stay here now will you please—,'

'Her belongings are in our room, her passport the lot, why would all that be there if she wasn't here!' argued Mikey.

Mikey went back to his hotel room and opened the safe, he was puzzled when he saw only his passport in the safe. He rushed to the suitcase, opened it looking for her passport he was more bewildered and shocked when he saw only his clothes in the suitcase and none of Rachel's! In a moment of panic he tipped it up, spilling all the clothes everywhere, he stripped the bed, opened the drawers, looked under the bed, turned the entire hotel room upside down in a desperate attempt to find Rachel's passport. 'This can't be happening!' He said to himself in a state of panic.

Alex was still stood by the bar in the hotel restaurant when Mikey come running in 'It's gone!' He said all panicky.

'What do you mean?' She asked him,

'Her passport is gone!!' Mikey claimed.

'Would she have it with her?' asked Alex,

'No I put both passports in the safe, Rachel's is gone, so are her clothes—,'

'Her clothes?' interrupted Alex.

'Yes!!' shouted Mikey, 'Everything of hers gone, someone's been in our room!!' He claimed.

'Why would someone break in, take her clothes and only her passport?' asked Alex,

'I don't fucking know!' shouted Mikey. Alex said nothing she just looked at Mikey.

'I'm sorry,' apologised Mikey feeling guilty for snapping at her,

'It's alright, what you wanna do?' asked Alex kindly.

Mikey looked around the marketplace he searched earlier this time tried asking stallholders if they had seen Rachel by showing his phone, many didn't understand him or they claimed to have not seen her. Suddenly, he spotted a woman stood alone with long dark hair and similar stature to Rachel, resembling her from behind. With a sense of relief, he moved over to her quickly, he soon stopped abruptly in his step as the woman turned around and it wasn't Rachel, Mikey sighed in disappointment.

Mikey tried the shop again he asked the staff working there if they had seen Rachel, again they hadn't. Mikey exited the shop, he walked further along the very noisy and busy with trucks and buses on the main road than he did earlier trying to find her. He asked in restaurants alongside the busy if anyone has seen Rachel, again no one had.

After hours of looking for Rachel, Mikey walked along a dirt track that ran behind the hotel, exhausted, aching, dehydrated and dripping in sweat from the heat of the burning hot sunshine raining mercilessly down on him. He resorted to shouting out her name. 'Rachel!!.....Rachel!!!' As he passed a makeshift shack, his shouting caused a local woman to come out and approach him. She began shouting at him in Thai. '*Why you shout like that! Fuck off!*' Mikey was oblivious to what she was saying

'Please have you seen this girl?' He tried to ask her whilst she continued to shout at him,

'*Go away, you come near hear you have problem!*' She shouted in Thai

'Please... you....' Mikey asked again trying to use hand gestures to explain what he meant, suddenly, out from the shack came a rough looking local man waving a metal pole, he struck Mikey hard on his arm, causing him to drop his phone, Mikey yelled in pain holding his arm, instantly he backed off, the man edged closer to Mikey.

'*Fuck off white man!*' He shouted in Thai and threatening with his metal pole. Mikey put his hands in front of him trying to imply he didn't want any trouble. He saw his phone on the floor he picked it up then turned and ran,

'*You come here again I kill you!*' The man shouted in Thai at Mikey as he quickly fled back to the hotel down the dirt track.

Back at the hotel, Alex stood near the bar counter when Mikey walked in holding his arm in pain 'Any luck?' She asked him,

'No!' snapped Mikey who carried on past her, Alex saw him holding his arm.

'What happened to you?' She asked him,

'Nothing!' snapped Mikey as he went to his room alone. Alex was baffled as to what happened to him.

In his hotel room, Mikey sat on the bed holding his arm. He took his hand away and saw a massive bruise on his arm from where the man with the metal bar hit him. 'That son of a bitch!' said Mikey angrily, he heard a knock on his room door, 'RACHEL!! He said and leapt up and ran to the door with a sense of optimism. His face soon turned back to disappointment when he opened the door and saw it was Alex not Rachel at the door. 'Oh sorry I'm not who you wanted it to be' said Alex as she followed Mikey into the room. She noticed the bruise on his arm. 'What's that from?' She asked him,

'Nothing,' said Mikey, I don't know what to do, do I get in touch with the embassy, do I go to the police? He said unsure what to do next.

'If she's left the hotel why would she take her passport and clothes?' asked Alex,

'I don't know,' replied Mikey 'I telling you someone has been in here and taken her stuff!' He insisted.

'But not yours?'

Mikey shook his head.

'This doesn't make sense.' said Alex all confused by everything Mikey has said and everything the hotel staff have claimed. Mikey looked at the time on his phone which said 17:00. 'Rachel's been missing since last night, I need to go to the police.' He said, he then got up and left.

Later that afternoon, Mikey entered the nearest police station, he walked up to the desk sergeant who was surrounded by piles and piles of paperwork and was too busy filling them out to notice Mikey. 'Excuse me, hello, excuse me I need to report someone missing,' he said trying to get the desk sergeant's attention, the desk sergeant didn't even acknowledge Mikey,

'Please take seat sir.' He muttered,

'This is urgent, please!' demanded Mikey, the desk sergeant stopped briefly and looked at Mikey,

'Take a seat someone will come see soon,' he said. Mikey looked and saw a busy packed waiting room filled with people waiting to see a police officer. He could not believe what he was seeing,

'You gotta be kidding me!' He said to himself. Mikey with no other option took a sat and waited to be seen, he looked up at the clock on the wall saying 17:45, Mikey waited, and waited, time went by the number of people in the waiting room didn't change as soon as a person left, another person arrived, Mikey waited and waited. Mikey looked at the clock again which now said 20:45, 3 hours had past and he still waited in the crowded waiting room to be seen, he was about to go ask the desk sergeant what was taking so long when a police officer came out of a room and asked who was next, finally, it was Mikey's turn, without hesitation he moved quickly to the police officer.

33

Mikey sat in the interview room with Inspector Sensit, a smartly dressed, but serious man in his mid 40s. He communicated to Mikey via a woman language translator. Mikey explained everything to the Inspector, who wrote notes, telling them the time he last saw Rachel, how she tried calling her, how no one else claimed to have seen her. Sensit spoke to Mikey via his translator. 'Do you have photo ID of her? Passport?' She asked him,

'No I said her passport is missing.' He said, before the translator could speak to Sensit,

'Wait!' Said Mikey, he remembered he had a photo of his and Rachel's passport numbers on his phone, what he had from booking the holiday. The translator and Sensit looked at Mikey as he scrolled through his phone. He showed Sensit and the translator the photo of Rachel's passport details. Sensit copied down the details.

'Thank you,' said the translator 'Do you have hotel address?' She asked him. Mikey pulled out a card with his hotel details from his phone case and handed it to the translator who handed it to Sensit. 'What happens now?' asked Mikey,

'We put this on file and be in touch soon.' replied the translator. Sensit and the translator packed up their files and stood up, 'Is that it?' asked Mikey not impressed by the polices effort.

'Yes sir, you go now.' replied the translator.

'Please you have to find her she's—,'

'Please sir we do our best.' interrupted the translator. Sensit held the door open for Mikey and spoke the only English word he knew, 'Goodbye.' He said. Mikey reluctantly left not really satisfied or hopeful with the police.

CHAPTER 5

B ack at the hotel, Mikey stood alone on the staircase staring out the open aimlessly into the pitch-black fields behind the hotel, the dirt track Mikey trekked up earlier went through the middle of the fields before disappearing into the cover of darkness. Alone, frightened, feeling lost, worried, the only company Mikey had was the small house lizards climbing the hotel walls and the crickets chirping a deafening sound in the fields below. Alex found Mikey stood there alone. 'What you doing here?' She asked him,

'I don't know,' said Mikey, 'I feel like I should be doing something but I don't know what to do!' He added.

'Did you go to the police?' She asked him, Mikey explained how he felt the police weren't interested, how he felt they would do nothing, he explained how he felt he hadn't done enough and didn't know what else to do.

'You've done more than enough, you don't have to be here alone either.' said Alex kindly.

Mikey & Alex both sat in Alex's hotel room. Mikey sat resting his head on his hands while Alex sat opposite him. 'Why did I leave her alone!' said Mikey feeling guilty,

'It's not your fault.' reassured Alex,

'All of this is, if I hadn't kept my trip secret from her we wouldn't be in this situation,' admitted Mikey,

'What secret trip?' asked Alex,

'Last night my best mate Joe text saying he booked rugby tickets for a weekend away we planned. Rachel happened to have my phone in her hand and saw the text.' explained Mikey,

'Didn't you tell her about the trip?'

'....No,' said Mikey,

'Why not?' asked Alex.

Mikey revealed how his relationship with Rachel has been very turbulent and testing at times for a long time, in particular because of his inability to keep a promise by not getting drunk when with his rugby friends, he revealed how the last time he went on a boozy weekend to Scotland with his best mate and friends it very nearly caused him and Rachel to break up as he was seen in the background of a Snapchat story photo chatting to a blonde girl, something which Rachel saw, and how he had to travel back home straight away in the early hours to save his relationship. He explained how a row he had with Rachel before he left prompted him to do so. Mikey admitted to how he gets carried away with drinking alcohol and it has caused many problems in their relationship. 'That sounds pretty steep.' said Alex taking it all in,

'We came here to try to rebuild our relationship,' explained Mikey, 'Yesterday everything was going perfect, I felt the happiest I've been for a long time. Now we have fallen out and I can't find her.' Mikey said with a tear in his eye. Alex leant across and touched his arm.

'You not to blame for any of this, you're doing everything right right now' she said kindly.

'Thanks for your help today Alex,' said Mikey feeling grateful.

'It's fine, if I was in your shoes I'd want all help I could get,' replied Alex.

'Do you have a partner?' Mikey asked her.

'No, got divorced and not bothered since, been there done that got the T-shirt.' She said.

'That's pretty steep too,' said Mikey,

'Ohhh yeah,' said Alex with a slight smirk 'It was, never going down that road again.' She added,

'That's a shame,' said Mikey,

'I'm not interested in that sort of thing anymore, besides it's irrelevant,' admitted Alex.

Mikey feeling restless got up. 'Where are you going?' Alex asked him,

'Need to look for her,' he replied,

'Mate it's late you should try to get some rest,' said Alex concerned.

'I can't sleep knowing Rachel is out there alone in a foreign country!' said Mikey.

'Let me come with you.' offered Alex. The two of them left her hotel room together.

Mikey and Alex split off in different directions along the busy main road Mikey had searched earlier, he checked in roadside restaurants, now full of other tourists, seeing other couples, both young and old sat together, happy and enjoying their holiday made Mikey feel emotional, as he knew that should be him and Rachel enjoying their holiday and each other's company. Mikey asked the staff again if any of them had seen Rachel, again all to no avail. Alex came back,

'Nothing down there,' she said, Any luck here?' She asked,

'No,' replied Mikey, 'I don't know where else to look!' He said with an upset tone in his voice,

'Maybe you should get some rest.' suggested Alex,

'What good is that gonna do?!' snapped Mikey, Alex put her hands on Mikey's shoulders,

'Mikey, I know this is really difficult for you, but you need rest, you have dark under your eyes, you're slurring your words, sleep deprivation is not good for the brain—,'

Mikey interrupted Alex, 'Oh so you're a doctor now are you?' He said sarcastically,

'I work in counselling and psychology so no, but l do know what I'm talking about.' replied Alex.

Mikey closed his eyes and sighed,

'I'm sorry,' he said,

'It's ok,' said Alex kindly, she hugged him,

'Let's go back to the hotel, get some rest and we'll look again soon,' she said, Mikey didn't answer her, 'The police will be looking for her as we speak, come on it's for the best.' Mikey reluctant to go back, agreed to do so.

Back in his hotel room, Mikey sat in the chair, he checked his phone every few seconds to see if Rachel had been touch, but nothing, Mikey spent the majority of the night awake, unable to just switch off and sleep knowing Rachel was missing.

The next day, Mikey with dark under his eyes from lack of sleep and still wearing the same clothes from two days ago sat in his hotel room chair nervously. Alex walked into his room. 'Hey' she said, she quickly peered into the hotel room bathroom then went over to Mikey. 'Anything?' She asked,

'No this is killing me' he replied, immediately he got up and headed for the door.

'Where are you going?' asked Alex following him. Mikey brisk walked down the corridors while Alex struggled to keep up with him.

'To the police, find any latest.' said Mikey.

'You gotta give the police time you only reported her missing last night,' advised Alex,

'So! They've had more than enough time to find something.' said Mikey,

'Wow wow stop stop,' said Alex as she stopped Mikey 'Look I know this must be real hard you but you going down there isn't gonna speed things up any quicker than they are now.' She advised.

Later that afternoon. Mikey and Alex sat in the reception hall, Mikey anxiously looked up at the entrance every time someone walked in. Fed up with waiting and feeling helpless he got up. 'Where you going?' asked Alex,

'Going into Bangkok to look for her.' said Mikey as he headed towards the hotel entrance,

'Mikey that's crazy you'll never find her there,' said Alex following him,

'I'll never find her just sat here!' stated Mikey,

'Mikey if you go into Bangkok and the police come you'll miss them,' warned Alex,

'I'll come straight back,' Mikey insisted,

'They won't wait for you,' warned Alex, 'I know it's frustrating we just have to wait, you've done everything you can,' she added.

'I haven't done enough.' claimed Mikey as he proceeded to walk out. As they approached the hotel entrance Alex held on to Mikey stopping him from going.

'No Mikey listen—,'

'Why are you trying to stop me?' He furiously asked her,

'I'm not you just gotta think logically—,'

'Would you sit here if it was someone you love?' asked Mikey, to which Alex didn't answer.

'Exactly!'

Mikey proceeded to walk off

'Mikey!' Alex called desperately to him, they both soon stopped when they saw Inspector Sensit, his translator and two uniformed policemen coming into the hotel. Inspector Sensit acknowledged Mikey.

Sensit, the translator, Mikey and Alex all sat in the restaurant. Sensit spoke to Mikey via his translator, 'We check with the airport there no record of Miss Moore leaving.' She said,

'Well at least we know she's still in the country,' said Alex,

Sensit spoke in Thai again.

'We no record of Miss Moore entering Thailand too,' said the translator, Mikey was gobsmacked as to what he'd just heard. Alex was surprised also,

'No we came here together!' Insisted Mikey, shocked at the revelation,

'Airport have no record of Miss Moore entering Thailand.' repeated the translator,

'No that ain't right you need to check that again!' asserted Mikey. Sensit spoke to Mikey, his translator spoke next,

'We ran both your passport numbers through the airport there is no record of Miss Moore entering Thailand only you sir.' She insisted.

Mikey was speechless,

'No Rachel was with me!' He insisted,

'That's got to be an error?' said Alex struggling to take in everything,

'No error, we check airport twice.' insisted the translator, Mikey shocked and gobsmacked began to panic,

'No this isn't happening!' He said. He stood up and began to wander backwards and forwards anxiously.

'Sir please remain calm.' said the translator,

'We went into Bangkok!' snapped Mikey, he got out his phone. 'I have photos of us here together!!' He stressed. Mikey scrolled through his photos on his phone, he was alarmed to see there are no photos of him and Rachel together on the holiday. Sensit and the translator looked at Mikey waiting for him to show them.

'No!!' cried Mikey,

'Now Mr Morris we—,'

'We checked into this hotel together!!' shouted Mikey, Sensit took a piece of folded paper from his file and placed it on the table. 'Sir will you please look at this,' Alex opened the folded paper, she gazed at it in surprise, she then looked at Mikey surprised.

'What?!' shouted Mikey, he came to the table and

opened the folded paper. He froze in horror when he saw a photo of only him and no Rachel, from the security footage at passport control at the airport.

Sensit spoke in Thai to Mikey.

'We requested footage of your arrival to make sure' said the translator, Mikey was in a state of shock at what he'd just seen, he shook with horror and began to breathe heavy.

'No......no.......no please this isn't right!' said a frightened Mikey,

'I'm sorry sir there's no record of—,'

'Stop saying that!!' interrupted Mikey shouting, 'Rachel was here you got to...' Mikey spotted a security camera above the reception desk. 'There!!' said Mikey pointing to it, Alex, Sensit, and the translator all looked up at the security camera. 'Check that! You will see me and Rachel arrive, together!' demanded Mikey, the translator spoke to Sensit.

'Well why not? You were able to check the airport!?' Suggested Alex.

Mikey, Alex, Wirat, Sensit, the translator and the two policemen all stood in Wirat's office, behind the reception desk looking at the hotel security camera screens. Chanchai put in a tape then fast-forwarded it to Mikey's arrival time then stopped the tape. 'This your time of arrival, yes?' asked Chanchai,

'Yes.' answered Mikey, Chanchai played the tape, everyone in the room watched it with their eyes glued to the screens. Mikey saw himself on the screen.

'There that's me, Rachel is just behind me,' he said, everyone continued watching the tape of Mikey checking in to the hotel. Mikey was confused as Rachel's was nowhere to be seen on the footage. He was horrified, as he saw himself on tape walk away from the reception desk alone. Sensit spoke in Thai to Mikey.

'We only see you?' said the translator, Alex was baffled too and looked at Mikey,

'No!! It's not possible!!' He ranted, 'I want to see a different camera!!' demanded Mikey,

'I don't see how that will help sir,' said Wirat,

'No!! I want to see a different camera!' Mikey demanded, 'Rachel was here!' He shouted.

'Sir please I—,'

'I can show you your arrival in taxi?' offered Chanchai,

'Yes!!..... please!' said Mikey,

the translator spoke in Thai to Sensit, he nodded his head in agreement. Chanchai put another tape into the machine then rewound it to show Mikey's arrival in the taxi 3 days ago. Chanchai played the footage. Everyone watched it, they saw the taxi Mikey arrived in, pull up outside the hotel, but they only saw Mikey get out of the taxi! Mikey was mortified, he held his hands over his head in shock. 'No! No! No!' he ranted,

Sensit spoke in Thai to Mikey.

Before the translator could speak, Mikey demanded to see another camera,

'Show me another camera!!'

Wirat had enough by now,

'Sir there is no point' he said,

Mikey didn't listen, in desperation he tried to mess with the hotel's security tapes and camera's himself.

'I wanna see another camera!' He demanded trying to play a tape,

'Mikey no!' shouted Alex as she and the two police officers tried to pull Mikey away as a struggle ensued.

Chanchai shouted at him in Thai ordering him to get off.

The two policemen grabbed Mikey and dragged him out of the office. Hotel guests in the hotels restaurant looked over at the commotion, the two policemen threw Mikey to the floor, he banged his knee on the hotel's hard floor. He held it in pain. Alex ran over to Mikey and crouched down to comfort him, she looked up at the police in disgust for being so brutal. Sensit, the translator and Wirat come out of the office.

Sensit spoke assertively in Thai to Mikey.

'The Inspector says Miss Moore is obviously not in the country therefore we will not be pursuing the case.' said the translator.

'Please! begged Mikey,

'He also says if you keep this up he will arrest you for wasting police time.' she warned.

Wirat angrily came over to Mikey, 'You continue to be problem I throw you out hotel!' He threatened. The police walked out of the hotel, Mikey having hurt his knee struggled to get up.

'No wait!!' He pleaded as he began to limp after them, but the police ignored him,

Alex tried holding him, 'Mikey',

'No wait why you doing this to me!! Please!! He pleaded trying to follow the police who ignored his pleas and left the hotel, Mikey stopped and lowered his head in his hands.

'She was here!!!' He shouted,

'Mikey come on' said Alex comforting him, Mikey cried on her shoulder as she consoled him.

'She was here!!' He cried as he sobbed.

Alex guided Mikey with her arm around him into her hotel room, Mikey traumatised by the whole event, was as white as a sheet as Alex guided him to the chair. 'You poor man, they had no right treating you like that!' said Alex kindly to him, still in a state of shock Mikey kept slowly repeating

'It's not possible, it's not possible.'

'Mikey,' said Alex sitting opposite him 'In my work as counselling, I deal with and listen to people who go through relationship or marital breakups, divorce, separations all that—,'

We haven't broken up! Mikey interrupted,

'Just here me out,' she said kindly, Mikey lost in trauma looked at Alex.

'A break up of a relationship or marriage can do serious psychological hurt to the mind,' she explained 'I have spent many hours listening to men and women who tell me after a traumatic break up they experience hallucinations of their partners to the extent they're so convinced they are there, then are completely surprised when they are suddenly not there,' Alex explained, Mikey couldn't believe what Alex was saying, was she trying to imply he imagined Rachel was with him?

'I did not imagine this!!' He snapped,

'These poor people are so convinced they go as far as booking restaurant tables for two or having a full-blown argument or conversation with just themselves thinking it's their other half, some of many delusions,' Alex explained 'This is called dissociative disorder, now the reason I'm telling you this from what I've seen and heard from you, and every proof of no one else seeing Rachel, footage of only you entering the hotel and the airport all contradict your claim, makes me strongly think you're suffering a form of this it's—,' before she could finish Mikey snapped

'Listen!' He shouted 'Rachel was here we—,'

'Mikey, there's no proof she was here,' interrupted Alex, 'I couldn't see any girly stuff in your hotel bathroom, you think a kidnapper is gonna take her clothes and a pack of tampons?!' She asked. Mikey looked in disbelief at Alex, why was Alex now siding with the hotel staff and the police in doubting him? Realising she had a point, he reluctantly agreed. 'You think I'm crazy?' He asked doubting his own mind.

'No, I resent using such term' said Alex 'No one is 'crazy' as most would describe, I prefer the term 'ill' as people can recover of this just the same way they can a sickness bug.' She explained.

'How does this help me? asked Mikey,

'I'll tell you, now before you came here did you and Rachel have a fight?'

Mikey thought back to the row he had with Rachel the morning after he came home drunk just over a week ago.

'.....Yes' he replied quietly,

'Was the fight a nasty one?' asked Alex, Mikey remembered himself and Rachel yelling and swearing at each other, he remembered Rachel in tears, Mikey remembered putting his fist through the wardrobe during the argument too. Mikey had a tear in his eye.

'...Yes.' He muttered

'Did it result in either you or Rachel leaving?' Alex asked him, Mikey remembered Rachel walking to the front door of their flat with her suitcase in tears and leaving him.

'..Yes.' He said, tears began to roll down his face as talking about it began to bring up painful and upsetting memories for him.

Alex explained more of the diagnosis to him, Mikey thinking back to how Rachel seem to vanish then reappear when he went into Bangkok, and the day he arrived at the hotel, he began to realise Alex may be right, he listened to her as she gave her professional opinion.

Mikey upset and with his head slouched slowly walked through the hotel bar, eyes of the hotel guests and staff, recognising him for the commotion earlier in the evening, star at him as he passed the restaurant and reception and headed towards the hotel entrance. In the pitch black of night, Mikey staggered out of the hotel, he stepped out into the very heavy downpour of rain, he stumbled down the road crying unfazed by the downpour, he stopped and kneeled down in the road, realising he must have been hallucinating Rachel being with him the entire time in Thailand, realising the hotel staff were correct, realising Rachel had left him before he came to Thailand, realising he has gone mad, he cried hysterically. Mikey's loud cries were heard by Sinh the hotel cleaner who lived in a shack next door to the hotel, he stood in his doorway and saw Mikey knelt down in the road crying and yelling, Sinh felt sorry for Mikey and walked over to him and wrapped him up in a blanket, and helped him up off the floor, too traumatised to notice where he was being taken Sinh guiding Mikey into his shack for shelter.

Mikey wrapped in the blanket, sat on an old broken wooden chair in a tiny one-room shack surrounded by empty whisky bottles and rubbish, a bucket filled with rainwater stood in the corner of the shack underneath a leak in the roof, all this was an apparent sign of Sinh's poverty. Sinh handed him a glass of whisky which he took Sinh sat down opposite on a broken, ripped old sofa. He spoke in a heavy Vietnamese accent. 'Why you cry?' He asked Mikey,

'I'm crazy.' replied Mikey staring a the floor,

'Where you from?' Sinh asked him,

'England.'

Sinh explained how during the Vietnam war an American bomb killed his family and left him badly disfigured, he went on to explain he went to America as an orphaned baby but was very badly abused by the American people for his disfigurement, and how he left but was not been able to go back to Vietnam, since then he's had a hatred of people since, and is very paranoid of English speaking people, especially Americans. Mikey said nothing, he slowly took a sip of his drink. 'Why you crazy?' asked Sinh,

'I don't know what's wrong with me!' said Mikey, 'I was so convinced my girlfriend was here, she's gone just like that. We broke up a week ago but I was convinced she was here with me no one has seen her, and I can't prove it! I just need to go home' he explained,

'Your lady pretty.' said Sinh,

'Yeah, she is,' answered Mikey thinking Sinh had asked him a question. 'I had it all and I blew it, now I'm going holidays where I think she's with me!' He said before downing his glass of whiskey.

'You look happy.' said Sinh,

'What do you mean?' asked Mikey unsure by what Sinh meant.

'I see you and your lady in hotel, you look happy.' Sinh replied. Mikey couldn't believe it! Someone else had seen Rachel?

'What!! Say that again?' He asked Sinh to make sure he heard correctly.

'I see you and your lady in hotel' Sinh repeated. Mikey was relieved and gobsmacked at what he'd just heard, he sat up with a new sense of hope.

'Oh my god, where is she? Have you seen her?' He asked Sinh,

'I no understand?' said Sinh who was confused by what Mikey was saying. Mikey stood up and approached Sinh,

'Oh please you have to help me, you need to tell them you saw her with me, please please!' He begged him, Sinh became agitated at Mikey's sudden persistence and began to shout at him in Thai, he quickly reached for a piece of metal, Mikey quickly backed off to avoid provoking him, and losing his only chance of finding Rachel.

'Alright, alright, alright, I'm sorry, I'm sorry ok, please I'm sorry!' said Mikey, Sinh glared a stern look at Mikey before putting the piece of metal down, Mikey explained everything to him how Rachel had been missing and no one claimed to have seen her, Sinh understood Mikey and agreed to accompany him to the police.

CHAPTER 6

Mikey and Sinh walked up to Alex's hotel room, 'Alex! Alex! It's Mikey, please open the door! Alex!' shouted Mikey as he banged on her door. Alex answered it.

'What is it?' She asked him,

'He's seen Rachel, we gotta go, we gotta—,'

'Wow wow slow down' interrupted Alex, 'What do you mean he's seen, Rachel?' She asked,

'He's the cleaner, he saw me and Rachel the day we arrived—,'

'Are you sure?' interrupted Alex,

'Yes!! We gotta go to the police now!' affirmed Mikey,

'Wait, show him the photo of Rachel' said Alex,

'What?' said Mikey,

'Show him the photo of Rachel,' said Alex,

'Why? We've gotta go now, come on!' demanded Mikey,

'Just do it!' insisted Alex,

'Fuck sake!' said Mikey as he got out his phone, he showed Sinh the photo of Rachel.

'Did you see this girl with Mikey?' Alex asked Sinh,

'Yes.' replied Sinh after he looked at the photo of Rachel on Mikey's phone.

'Ok let's go.' agreed Alex.

Mikey, Alex & Sinh approached the reception desk where Chanchai was sat. 'Can you order us a taxi?' asked Alex,

'Where you going?' asked Chanchai,

'Police station, this man has seen the missing girl,' replied Alex, Chanchai was surprised by Alex's claim, knowing that Sinh had a drink problem, he tried to convince them that Sinh couldn't be trusted,

'This man drinks you can no believe what he say—,'

'Can you just do it!' interrupted Mikey impatiently, Chanchai said nothing then offered them all a lift with the hotel's shuttle car.

'Please, we have driver available let us take you.' He said,

'That'd be great.' said Mikey who started to feel a sense of hope at last.

Chanchai shouted in Thai to Love and ordered him to fetch the hotel car.

The hotel shuttle car pulled up outside the hotel's front entrance, the heavy downpour of rain continued to lash down, Mikey, Alex and Sinh quickly got in to avoid getting soaked, Love was sat in the driver's seat. Everyone listened as the rain pounded the roof of the car, Chanchai unexpectedly came and sat in the front passenger seat. Mikey was puzzled as to why Chanchai was joining them. 'He no know way to police,' explained Chanchai,

'Oh right ok,' said Mikey thinking no more of it. The car set off on its way. Chanchai spoke in Thai to Sinh,

'Sinh, you saw his girlfriend yes?'

Sinh replied in Thai he did,

'*Ok*' replied Chanchai in Thai, suddenly, he pulled out a gun and shot Sinh dead! Alex screamed in fright, the gunshot startled her and blood from the wound splattered on her. Mikey froze in horror at what he just witnessed.

The hotel shuttle car driven by Love, drove along the dirt track behind the hotel. The car pulled up at a construction site. Chanchai holding a gun got out the passenger door, unfazed by the heavy rain he opened the side door and aimed his gun at Mikey and Alex. 'Get out!' He ordered them, Mikey and Alex with no other option got out slowly and nervously with their hands up. Love come running round to Chanchai from the driver seat. Chanchai threw Love some cable ties whilst pointing his gun at Mikey and Alex, speaking in Thai, he ordered Love to tie their hands together, Love tied Alex's hands first then went to Mikey's hands, due to the rain making his hands and the cables slippery and being under pressure to do it quickly he accidentally dropped them which infuriated Chanchai, who blasted him for taking so long, eventually he did. Chanchai aiming his gun at Mikey & Alex ordered them into the construction site.

Alex and Mikey walked through the construction site in total darkness as the place had no light, nor were there any street lights, tripping over or catching their footing on scattered building materials and tools left lying around. Chanchai and Love escorted them into an unfinished room with a trap door in the middle of the floor, Love switched on a builders light, its brightness dazzled Mikey and Alex briefly. 'What do you want with us!' asked a frightened Alex,

'Shut up!!' shouted Chanchai aiming his gun at both Mikey & Alex stood in the middle of the room. Chanchai gave more cable ties to Love and ordered him to tie Mikey's & Alex's hands to the metal rebar's coming poking out of the concrete. Love does so then stood next to Chanchai who lowered his gun. 'You stupid arsehole, you just couldn't take the hint.' He taunted Mikey,

'What are you talking about?' Asked Mikey,

'You want see her so badly?' Chanchai taunted, he nodded to Love who opened the trap door before going into it. Mikey & Alex watched as Love disappeared out of sight, only to reappear moments later dragging out Rachel!

'Rachel!' shouted Mikey,

'Oh my god!' said Alex in shock as she realised Mikey was telling the truth the entire time. Rachel with her hands tied behind her, wearing the same dress she wore when she & Mikey visited Bangkok was all ripped and torn, her arms and legs were covered in dirt and bruised, was dragged out by Love and he placed her in the middle of the room, she shook with fear as she looked around, Mikey furiously tried to break himself free.

'What the fuck have you done to her!' He shouted,

'Shut up!' shouted Chanchai,

'What do you want with her!' shouted Mikey as he tried to break free, Chanchai walked over to Mikey and punched him in the stomach, the punch winded Mikey, causing him to collapse to his knees. 'Stop!!!' begged Alex,

Mikey struggled for breath, Chanchai walked over to Rachel. Mikey looked to Chanchai and Love. 'Alright

alright let them go, leave me, just please let them go.' pleaded Mikey,

'He say shut up!' said Love,

'You pathetic!' Taunted Chanchai, he squatted down next to Rachel, he rubbed his fingers through her hair,

'Pretty girl, I show her real man!!' He taunted, he then dragged her across the floor to the corner of the room.

'No please! No please!' begged Rachel,

'Leave her alone!' begged Mikey,

'No don't do it!' pleaded Alex.

To silence everyone's shouting, Chanchai fired his gun at the wall between Mikey and Alex, the gunshot frightened them both.

'Quiet bitch, you're next!' He said tauntingly to Alex. Chanchai sat on top of Rachel, he ripped her dress nearly exposing her breasts, she cried, Love looked away uncomfortably, Mikey, Alex and Rachel all pleaded with Chanchai, Mikey desperately tried yanking his hands, hoping to snap the cable ties to get free. Chanchai looked at Mikey with a sardonic grin at what he was about to do, he looked back at Rachel, he positioned himself on her,

'No!!' begged Mikey feeling helpless,

suddenly, everyone heard a voice from outside shout.

'Chanchai!' called the voice,

Chanchai stopped what he was about to do to Rachel and looked towards the door. Love looked to the door too. The man walked in, Mikey and Alex were horrified to see it was Inspector Sensit!

'You!!' said a shocked Mikey,

'Oh my god!' said Alex who was also shocked too, Sensit shouted in Thai at Chanchai,

'*How many times do I have to tell you, the girls are not to be touched until Tripput takes them!*' Chanchai sighed then stood up and walked to Sensit,

'*Why you shoot the man? I said any problem you bring them to me!!*' shouted Sensit in Thai, he then slapped Chanchai for killing Sinh, as that left a problem for them,

'*Fucking idiot!*' Sensit said in Thai,

'*Get off!*' answered back Chanchai in Thai, the two men argued amongst themselves.

'You knew the whole time!!' shouted Mikey, Sensit replied in English, revealing he could speak English after all.

'Shut up you should have gone home when you had the chance!' He said to him,

'What the hell do you want with us!!' Mikey shouted, 'Let them go I'll stay just let them go, please!' He pleaded,

'You're all coming with us!' said Sensit,

'I will go with you, let them both go they've done nothing wrong—,'

'No she has seen too much,' Sensit interrupted as he looked towards Alex, he ordered Love to cut her loose, before getting out his gun. Love picked up a sharp rusty piece of metal and cut Alex free, Sensit grabbed Alex by her arm and dragged her out the room at gunpoint.

'Where you taking her!' shouted Mikey, Sensit ignored Mikey and forced Alex into another room at gunpoint,

'Stand over there!' He ordered her, shoving her against the wall. Alex stood by the wall then slowly turned and faced Sensit with her hands up. Mikey still tied to metal begged Chanchai & Love,

'Don't hurt them let them both go!' He pleaded as couldn't see where Sensit had taken Alex. In the next room,

Sensit mercilessly aimed his gun at Alex, tears filled her eyes as she knew her fate was sealed. BANG!! In the other room, Mikey startled as he heard the gunshot coming from the next room. 'No!!!!' shouted a devastated Mikey, Love cut Mikey loose, he ran over to Rachel, before he could get to her Chanchai shoved Mikey away from her then aimed his gun at him.

'Stand still!' He shouted, Mikey angrily and reluctantly complied.

'You sick bastards!!' He shouted,

Chanchai pushed and held Mikey against the wall, he put the barrel of his gun in Mikey's mouth, Mikey gagged and choked as the gun was pressed against his throat.

'I will fucking kill you! Shut up!' threatened Chanchai, Sensit walked back in and ordered Love & Chanchai to take Mikey & Rachel outside. Chanchai took his gun out of Mikey's mouth, Mikey coughed and gasped for breath, the taste of gun residue lingered in his mouth, he spat out blood as the front iron sights from Chanchai's gun had cut inside the top of his mouth, he looked up to see Love drag Rachel off the floor and escort her out the room.

'Where you taking her!' He shouted, Chanchai escorted him out at gunpoint. Whilst Mikey was escorted out they passed the next room and he saw Alex's body lying on the floor.

'Alex! Alex!' Mikey called to her, Alex's lifeless body just lay still and silent.

Mikey and Rachel were escorted out of the construction site in the heavy downpour of rain by Love and Chanchai, Chanchai ordered Love to get the car, Love failed to hear

Chanchai and looked back at him confused when he misunderstood his instructions. With their backs turned, Mikey and Rachel seized their chance and made a run for it! Chanchai berated Love for them getting away before chasing after them on foot himself. Love called for Sensit, who came rushing from the construction site, he slammed Love for the mishap and ordered him to get the car. Chanchai chased Mikey & Rachel down the dirt track which ran parallel to the fields of tall grass, which were located behind the hotel.

Chanchai caught up with them, he pushed Rachel, with her hands still tied behind her, unable to stop herself, she fell to the floor cutting her chin, Chanchai then kicked Mikey in the back of his legs, causing him to fall. Rachel hurt from her fall struggled to get up, Chanchai pointed his gun at her.

'Don't move you stupid bitch!' He shouted, Rachel in fear stopped.

Mikey attempted to get back up too, Chanchai suddenly struck him across the face with the butt of his gun.

'No!!' Rachel cried as Mikey fell back to the floor, he attempted to get back up whilst holding his face in pain, Chanchai pointed his gun close to Mikey's face, Rachel watched in horror, Chanchai smirking side eyed a stunned Rachel,

'Say goodbye to your ma—,'

suddenly, Chanchai was pummelled to the ground, as Mikey rugby tackled him, his grip on the gun loosened as it sailed into the tall grass. Sensit and Love still near the construction site jerked their heads toward the commotion. Mikey & Chanchai exchanged punches,

'Rach run!!' shouted Mikey as he fought with Chanchai, Rachel hesitated for a moment then limped away for cover.

Mikey & Chanchai continued to fight, although Mikey was taller, Chanchai was physically stronger and knew how to fight, Mikey tried to hold Chanchai so Rachel could get away, Chanchai desperately wriggled himself of Mikey's grasp and managed to get his hand around Mikey's throat. Mikey began to choke and gurgle for breath. From a short distance, Sensit, aimed his gun at Mikey, the heavy downpour and rainwater on the gun's iron sight made visibility and aiming hard. Sensit squinted and steadied his gun. Mikey was close to passing out from Chanchai's grip around his throat, heard a gunshot. Suddenly Chanchai's grip around Mikey's throat loosened, Chanchai fell to the floor as Sensit accidentally shot Chanchai instead of Mikey, Mikey sucked in a mouthful of air, upon seeing Sensit & Love running towards him, clutching his bruised throat, Mikey scrambled for cover in the tall grass. Sensit and Love approached Chanchai's body. Sensit swore in frustration at killing Chanchai, he then ordered Love to find Rachel, the two of them split off searching.

Mikey hid in the tall grass, from his hiding spot, Sensit's shoes crackled under dead grass, unknowingly approaching him. Mikey shut his eyes tight and held his breath as the sound of crackling grass from Sensit's footsteps grew closer, and closer, Mikey held his eyes shut extremely tight, as Sensit came within inches of him, then, the sound of crackling grass began to subside, descending faintly into the distance, as Sensit walked away. He opened his eyes, breathed a sigh of relief. His relief was short lived as he rolled onto his side, he froze in horror as a giant Burmese Python snake slowly slithered across his leg! Petrified, Mikey did not move a muscle. Eventually, the snake moved on, Mikey breathed a huge sigh of relief before moving away. He desperately tried to find Rachel, he couldn't call out to her as Sensit & Love would hear him, he had to slouch and remain out of sight in case Sensit & Love saw him, all this in a field of tall grass now home to what could be hundreds of dangerous snakes as well!

Love waded through the tall grass, he stumbled upon Rachel cowering in fear and hiding. He shouted to Sensit, suddenly, out of the tall grass Mikey rugby tackled Love to the ground. Sensit looked behind him after hearing Love shout. Love, not being as physically strong as Chanchai, was quickly overpowered by Mikey, he punched Love in the face, breaking his nose, Mikey grabbed Rachel, the two ran, BANG!! They dived into the tall grass to hide again after hearing Sensit's gunshot. Sensit waded through the tall grass found Love on the floor in agony holding his bleeding nose. Sensit unsympathetically dragged him up and ordered him after Mikey and Rachel. Mikey & Rachel crawled slowly through the tall grass, Mikey crawled to the grass verge by the dirt track, he stopped at the feet of Sensit. He looked up at Sensit mercilessly pointing his gun to his face, Sensit nearly squeezed the trigger when, suddenly, he was struck from behind by a metal pole by the local man who threatened Mikey the day before. The man struck Sensit again, unintentionally saving Mikey's life. Sensit fell to the floor unconscious, Mikey and Rachel got up, the local man saw Mikey then swung his metal pole at him, Mikey ducked and grabbed Rachel, the two ran down the dirt track, the local man chased them so far shouting at them in Thai before stopping.

Mikey & Rachel ran to the road where the hotel was, they squatted down behind a wall to hide. 'Is he there?' asked a scared Rachel,

'I don't know!' replied Mikey, suddenly the young terrified couple were blinded by headlights and blue flashing lights coming towards them. Rachel hid her face behind Mikey.

'Oh my gosh what is it!!' She asked him,

'It's ok it's ok' said Mikey realising it was the police. Love came running onto the road he stopped when he saw Mikey and Rachel, he took a step toward them then stopped when he saw the blue flashing lights, realising the game was up, Love put his hands up to surrender.

CHAPTER 7

The next day, Rachel lay in a hospital bed, Mikey sat next to her, he refused treatment for the cut on his face as he refused to leave Rachel's side. He sat with his elbow's leant on the bed, resting his head on his hands, he watched over Rachel as she slept. Still on edge and jumpy, Mikey startled and quickly looked up every time a doctor or nurse or anyone came onto the ward. Now the adrenaline had calmed down, Mikey's eyes soon filled with tears as he had time to reflect on the ordeal over the past few days. Feeling guilty and responsible for everything that happened to Rachel, he cried, he held Rachel's hand as she slept, 'I'm sorry,' he sobbed, 'I'm so so sorry,' he said with tears rolling down his face. Mikey leant forward onto the bed, he kissed Rachel's hand and held it tight. Rachel opened her eyes slightly, she heard Mikey crying as he buried his face into the bed, she smiled as she felt safe with him there with her before going back to sleep. Mikey having not slept properly for days, finally gave in to his exhaustion and fell asleep beside Rachel.

Hours passed, Mikey woke up on the hospital ward, he sat up, he saw Rachel was no longer in the bed! He looked all around the ward, only to see it was in darkness and completely empty! Mikey began to panic, he leapt out of the chair and made his way towards the corridor heading out of the ward, the corridor was long and empty, not a sole was about, he ran the length of the corridor, he stopped abruptly and turned around, to his horror, at the other end of the corridor was Inspector Sensit!! Sensit grinned at him before heading onto the ward, 'No!!' shouted Mikey as he ran back down the corridor fearing for Rachel, he ran back into the ward where Chanchai, Love & Sensit were stood around the empty ward, Rachel was nowhere to be seen! 'Where is she?!' Mikey shouted,

'Sir, sir, sir' replied Love,

Mikey startled and woke up to the nudging off a hospital nurse

'sir, sir?' She said,

Mikey quickly looked up, Rachel was still asleep in the bed, the ward still had other patients in, Mikey breathed a huge sigh of relief as it was only a dream.

'Are you ok sir?' asked the nurse,

'How long was I asleep?' Mikey asked her,

'Only minutes, you were shaking very badly,' she explained, Mikey rubbed his eyes and took a big breath.

'Can I get you anything sir?' asked the nurse,

'No, Thanks.' said Mikey.

The nurse turned to walk away,

'Wait!' called Mikey, the nurse turned to him, 'Have you had an Australian woman in here? Her name's Alex?' He asked, the nurse looked puzzled at Mikey,

'Tall, blonde, Australian, do you understand me?' asked Mikey,

'Sorry sir I don't know.' replied the nurse who then left.

Mikey sat back in the chair, disappointed and upset not knowing if Alex was rescued.

One week later. Having been discharged from hospital and been interviewed by the police, Mikey and Rachel both sat at a table at the British embassy in Bangkok. Sir Philip Lawrence, The British Ambassador to Thailand, he was a man in his early 60s, dressed in a suit, he walked into the room, he was accompanied by Edwards, a serious looking man in his late 30s, his was an officer from Interpol, dressed in black. 'Good morning, Sir Philip Lawrence, I'm the British Ambassador to Thailand. How are you both?' said Sir Philip introducing himself. The two men sat opposite them. 'This is Edwards, from Interpol's Bangkok office,' said Sir Philip introducing the man with him. Edwards acknowledged Mikey & Rachel.

'Edwards just wants to ask you a few questions' explained Sir Philip, 'I'm sorry to put you through it all again.' He said kindly.

Edwards put some photos of Chanchai, Love and Sensit on the table.

'Chanchai Chairat, Love Ahuja and Inspector Sensit are members of the insurgency group National Front of Yata, they were all under the command of this man.' He explained before showing them a photo of another man. 'Did you see this man at all?' He asked Mikey & Rachel, Mikey looked at the photo and recognised him as the man who entered the hotel the night he and Rachel sat in the hotel restaurant, the day they arrived at their hotel.

'He called into the hotel the day we arrived, who is he?'

asked Mikey, 'Chakrii Tipput, a well-known commander of Yata, one of many groups battling Thai forces on the border with Malaysia. He has been on Interpol's list for some time and these men were some of his many associates' explained Edwards, Mikey shook his head in disbelief.

'They had me convinced Rachel wasn't here,' explained Mikey 'They had it on camera, at the airport, I genuinely thought I was crazy I—,'

'I read your Police statements,' interrupted Edwards, 'Turns out Chanchai Chairat was an expert in camera manipulation, and Love Ahuja admitted to drugging you with a sleeping pill, I guess that explains why they were able to be a step ahead of you on the night. As for the airport security footage and immigration system we can only assume Tipput and Sensit have friends in the airports. No one really knows who else is involved with Tipput or Yata.' He went on to explain.

Mikey was shocked at what he's just heard. Rachel got tears in her eyes as talking about it become upsetting for her.

'I'm sorry Miss Moore I understand this must be really difficult for you, for both of you.' said Sir Philip very sympathetically.

Mikey put his arm around her, 'It's ok, we're safe here,' he said, 'Any word on Alex?' He asked Sir Philip & Edwards,

Edwards shook his head in response,

'I'm afraid we don't have that information sorry.' said Sir Philip. Mikey covered his eyes with his hand and sighed with disappointment.

'I understand Miss Cahill was of some assistance to you?' asked Sir Philip,

'Yes!' said Mikey feeling guilty,

'I'm sorry.' apologised Sir Philip,

Mikey looked down at the table in sadness, he felt guilty and responsible for Alex's death, Rachel held his hand.

'You'll be pleased to know you're booked on the next flight back to London, you're going home.' explained Sir Philip,

'Thank you.' said Mikey.

Sir Philips handed Mikey & Rachel their flight documents.

Edwards picked up the photos and his file.

'It's the least I can do, and I am sorry for what you both have had to go through, take care.' said Sir Philip before leaving with Edwards.

Mikey wondered for a moment then got up and chased after them, Rachel was puzzled as to where he was going.

'Wait!' He called to Sir Philip & Edwards who stopped and turned around to Mikey. 'I don't get it, why? Was it ransom they were after?' Mikey asked them,

'No, these sick bastards kidnap women purely for sexual slavery, western women have a higher value it's all just one sick trade,' said Edwards, 'Sadly it's widely forgotten about the hundreds of local young girls and women that have gone missing too.' He explained.

Mikey couldn't believe what he just heard.

'This has happened before?' He asked.

'Regretfully yes, a French couple on their honeymoon, the wife suddenly disappeared, all denied her existence to her husband. It's also tragic the husband got himself killed trying to find her.' Edwards explained.

Mikey could not believe what he just heard,

'Why is none of this reported?!' He asked,

'Look these criminals have links all over the Far East, in government, everywhere.' admitted Edwards 'It's very easy to cover your tracks and deny such a problem exists when you have friends in high places. A problem that would put off the tourist's, something Thailand depends on. Unfortunately corruption is very rampant in this part of the world.' Edwards explained,

Mikey looked behind him to the room where Rachel was sat, realising how bad and widespread the organisation is, and how lucky he was to find Rachel before she would have disappeared for good. 'Looks like in your case the two at your hotel failed to take into account the cleaner would blow their cover' added Edwards.

'Take care Mr Morris.' said Sir Philip as he left with Edwards.

Later that day, Mikey and Rachel made their way through the crowded airport to finally go home, Mikey was very paranoid after the ordeal, he refused to leave Rachel's side. Mikey and Rachel were about to set off for security when they heard a woman's voice shout at them. They turned around, and to their delight, they saw Alex in the crowd stood by the check-in queues smiling. Overcome with joy, they rushed over to her and hugged.

'I'm so glad you're ok!' said Mikey relieved to see Alex was alive.

'Yeah luckily didn't hit anything vital, hospital wanted me to stay longer but I just want to go home.' She said,

'That's great! Thank you, Alex thank you for everything' said a grateful Mikey.

'Not at all, take care of yourselves, keep in contact!' said Alex,

'Free holiday to Oz!' joked Mikey, winking at Rachel who just smiled.

'Why not!!' laughed Alex, 'You got a good man their hun' she said to Rachel,

Rachel looked at Mikey, smiled and rubbed his arm. 'Yeah.' She said happily,

Mikey put his arm around Rachel.

'Safe travels' said Mikey,

'You too, Pom!' joked Alex,

'You'd be a Pom if your ancestors weren't criminals,' joked Mikey,

'Ay now now,' laughed Alex,

'Take care Alex' said Mikey,

'You too.' replied Alex, Mikey and Alex hugged each other once more before he and Rachel left for the airport's gate. They both waved to Alex as they made their way up the airport escalator towards security. Alex smiled and waved back, her face soon turned to a look of disgust and anger as Mikey & Rachel disappeared into the crowd of people heading towards the security section.

At the airport gate, Mikey and Rachel sat waiting to board their plane, whilst Mikey waited, he took a moment to reflect on how much hurt and anger had gone on before in his relationship with Rachel, after realising how he nearly lost Rachel for good, he vowed to himself things would be different from now on, this time he was going to stick to that pledge no matter what. He & Rachel both took a moment and shared an emotional hug, after realising how much they nearly lost each other. Although Mikey didn't say it out loud how things would change with him, Rachel knew things would be different from now on, and she knew it would be for definite this time. She also realised very early on that Mikey really did love her, as he didn't give up in his search for her, how he put his own life on the line trying to find her and save her. Mikey looked at his phone and saw he had a text from Joe, which read: 'Did you get my message?' To which he replied 'Yes, I'm not coming.' He sent it then switched the phone off.

'Who's that? asked Rachel,

'No one just switching it off.' Mikey replied. He put his arm around Rachel they smiled at each other as they joined the queue to board their plane home. The pair arm in arm stepped onto their plane, the crowd of passengers in front of them stopped as a family struggled to put their hand luggage in the overhead cabinet,

'What's the holdup?' asked Mikey,

'Probably gormless people looking for headphones again.' replied Rachel, Mikey and Rachel both smiled at each other and lovingly rested their foreheads together smiling.

CHAPTER 8

Back downstairs in the airport, Alex stood in the busy crowd, spotted a young beautiful woman and her boyfriend of similar age, both of whom were from Russia, they were stood at a kiosk browsing hotels. The woman went to the kiosk desk, Alex approached her boyfriend.

'Hi are you looking for a hotel?' She asked him, the man who didn't know much English nodded his head. Alex handed him a leaflet for a hotel.

'I just come from here, it's really nice, got a pool and it's really close!' She said,

the man took the leaflet and flicked through it, he smiled with impression. The hotel in the leaflet was the same one Mikey & Rachel stayed at!

'Thank you.' said the man in a thick Russian accent, 'Pleasure, you'll really like it.' said Alex before she departed when the man's girlfriend turned to come back. Alex stood aside then turned around, she watched the couple both look at the leaflet and then leave. Alex reached into her handbag and got her phone out when she saw the couple were out of sight.

'Yeah it's me a couple on route to you now, I'll be there

tonight.' She said on the phone, Alex put her phone away, she smirked as she had set a trap for the couple.

Later that day, Alex arrived back at the hotel, she spotted the couple she clocked at the airport leaving the hotel's restaurant, Alex quickly turned her head away to avoid eye contact. Alex walked over to the reception desk where she acknowledged Asnee, he was an athletic man of average height in his early 30s and the new hotel concierge. Asnee stood up and walked into Wirat's office behind the reception desk, Alex followed him. Asnee & Alex watched the couple walk through the hotel on the hotels CCTV till they entered their hotel room. Asnee switched on his laptop, through a hidden camera in their hotel room, Alex & Asnee were able to watch the Russian couple in their room. The pair studied the couple. 'No fuck ups this time!' Insisted Alex 'Those Pommy fuckers were lucky!' She explained.

'What is Pommy?' Asked Asnee.

'Doesn't matter, there cannot be any slip ups this time.' said Alex.

'Yes.'

'And make sure the new cleaner is either on board or silenced as well!' affirmed Alex.

'Yes, don't worry, we be careful this time.' replied Asnee.

Alex looked seriously at Ansee hoping he was right.

'Anyone else?' asked Alex, Ansee flicked to another hidden camera on his laptop, the screen showed another hotel room with another young woman sat on the bed on her own.

'Her,' said Ansee

'And?'

'She travel alone, she from Denmark.' said Ansee

'Good, at least don't have a boyfriend or husband to deal with.' said Alex. Ansee closed his laptop, 'I'm going, stick to the plan,' said Alex, 'Oh and remember, you don't know me!' She reminded Ansee.

'Yes.' He replied as Alex left the office.

The next morning, Alex left her hotel room, she made her into the hotel restaurant for breakfast. As she sat in the restaurant she the Russian man, whom she followed from the airport, wandering around the hotel bar alone, appearing look all around as if he was looking for somebody. Alex got her phone out of her handbag and saw she had a message which read: 'We have girl' she smirked as she read the message. As she put her phone away, she noticed the man arguing with Wirat and Ansee and the new hotel waiter. Seeing this was now her opportunity, she got up from her table and approached and him, 'Hi, we met at the airport!' She said.

EPILOGUE

The next day, back in the cold miserable rain soaked winter of England, Mikey and Rachel's plane landed at Heathrow Airport in London. As the pair made their way through the busy with people arrivals terminal and the immigration desks, Rachel's parents were waiting for the couple. Rachel saw them, overcome with emotion, she ran to her parents and hugged them both, her mother held her tightly and lovingly, her father shook Mikey's hand and thanked him for everything he'd done, as well as forgiving him for everything that had gone on before, her mother gratefully hugged and embraced him, with tear in her eye she held his hand. Whilst Mikey & Rachel stood with her parents, an South East Asian looking man stood behind a pillar in the arrivals hall, the huge crowd of people made his hiding easier. He watched the family embrace each other, as the four of them proceeded to leave the arrivals hall, the man keeping slight distance followed them!

THE END.

Lightning Source UK Ltd.
Milton Keynes UK
UKHW010859100921
390347UK00002B/324